The Andersuns: Jarrell's Sweet Tooth

E. Diann Cook

AuthorHouse™
1663 Liberty Drive
Bloomington, IN 47403
www.authorhouse.com
Phone: 1-800-839-8640

First published by AuthorHouse 12/31/2009

ISBN: 978-1-4490-4997-3 (sc)

Library of Congress Control Number: 2009912608

Contact Information

http://www.dijarodesigns.com
dijaro designs
P.O. Box 320181
Hartford, CT 06132 - 0181
dijarodesigns@yahoo.com

Illustrations, story, lyrics, and song by E. Diann Cook
Music composed by Paul H. Cameron, Sr.

Printed in the United States of America
Bloomington, Indiana

This book is printed on acid-free paper.

This book is dedicated with loving memories to Kenneth H. Alston

Kenny,

without you putting forth *the question*, I might not have sought *the answer.*

Thank you for sharing and being the "sunshine" of my life.

Acknowledgments

GOD – Thank you for everything. Amen!

Faith S.D.A. Church – Thank you for giving me the platform to premiere my stories.

Family – Thank you for always using the bottom line to push me to the top. Especially my son, JaVon, who is a creative talent in his own right. I know you will surpass even your own expectations.

Friends – Thank you for caring enough to support yet another vision.

Ben Andersun is the dad.

Mae Andersun is the mom

Shana Andersun is their oldest child and is seventeen years old.

JaVon Andersun is their oldest son and is sixteen years old

Thomas Andersun is their thirteen year old son.

Keturah and Jarrell Andersun are their eight year old twins

Jarrell Andersun

Tamanique Andersun is the two year old baby of the family.

Tailor is the family's shaggy dog.

Jarrell Andersun
had a sweet tooth.
A big sweet tooth.

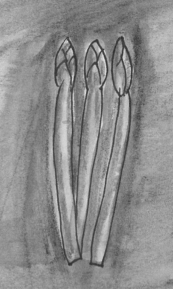

He liked cakes and candy,

pie and ice cream,

cookies and cupcakes.

Yes, everything sweet.

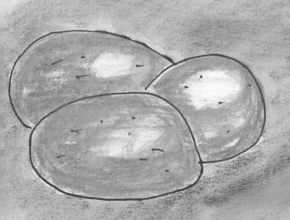

His mom always had a hard time getting him to eat a good, healthy meal. For breakfast, his mom made oatmeal and toast, or turkey bacon and eggs, or pancakes and sausage.

But Jarrell always asked for cakes and candy, pie and ice cream, cookies and cupcakes.

Yes, everything sweet.

Of course, his mom said, "No sweets for breakfast, dear. Eat your eggs, toast, and banana so you can grow strong and healthy."

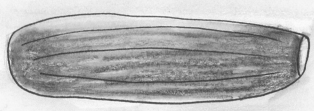

When it was lunchtime, Jarrell asked, "Mommy, can we have cakes and candy, pie and ice cream, cookies and cupcakes?"

His mom replied, "No sweets for lunch, dear. Eat your soup and sandwich so you can grow strong and healthy."

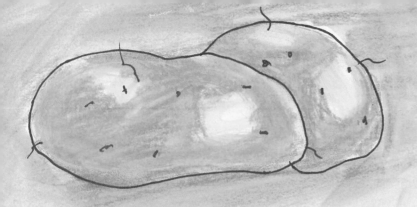

This happened a lot, until one day, Jarrell decided not to eat his dinner, because there were no sweets.

He was sent to his room to think about the choice he had made.

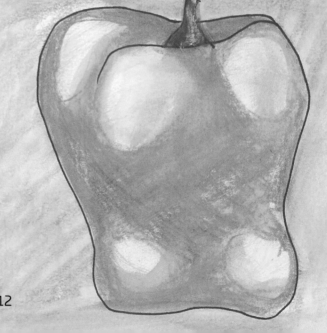

Jarrell was determined not to change his mind and fell asleep saying,

"I want cakes and candy, pie and ice cream, cookies and cupcakes. Yes, everything sweet."

Morning came, and Jarrell heard his mom calling, "Jarrell, breakfast is ready!" Jarrell got up and walked downstairs to the kitchen.

When he got there, he looked at the table and shouted, "Wow!"

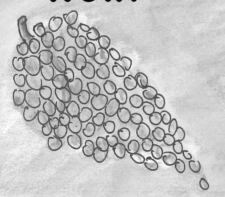

He saw cakes and candy, pie and ice cream, cookies and cupcakes, and everything sweet!

He laughed
and said,
"Mommy is
this really
breakfast?"

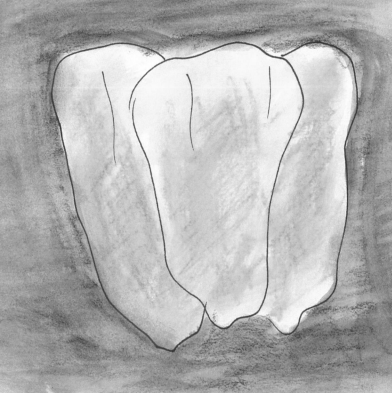

His mom said,
"Yes, dear.
Isn't this what
you've always
wanted?"

"Thank you,
Mommy, thank
you!" cheered
Jarrell.

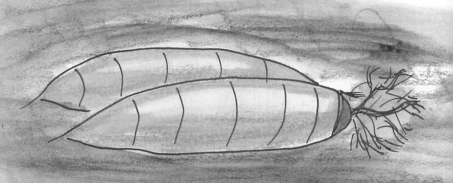

He ate and ate and ate,
until he ate everything.

"Did you have enough,
dear?" asked his mom.

"Yes, Mom," Jarrell answered,
rubbing his stomach.

But Jarrell didn't feel
well, so he went back
to his room to lie
down for a while.

He fell asleep, and when he woke up, he heard his mother calling, "Jarrell, breakfast is ready!"

Jarrell realized he had been dreaming and that his mom would not give him cakes and candy, pie and ice cream, cookies and cupcakes for breakfast.

So he jumped out of bed and ran downstairs, but when he got to the table guess what he saw?

Cakes and candy,
pie and ice cream,

cookies and cupcakes!

Jarrell let out
a big scream:
"Ahhhhhh!"

He closed his eyes, and when he opened them, he was back in his bedroom and his mom was calling him.

"Jarrell, breakfast!"

Was this another dream?
He didn't know what to do.

His mother called again,

so he got out of bed and slowly walked downstairs. He looked on the table— and what do you think he saw?

Eggs, sausage,
toast, and orange juice.
Jarrell gave his mom a big
hug and a smile.
"Mommy," he said, "I
had a dream. It started
out so good."

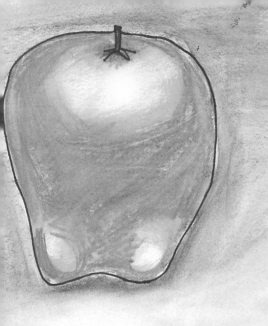

"You made me cakes and candy, pie and ice cream, cookies and cupcakes, and everything sweet, just like I always wanted."

"But eating all of those sweets made my stomach hurt. I think I'll eat what you make from now on, Mommy."

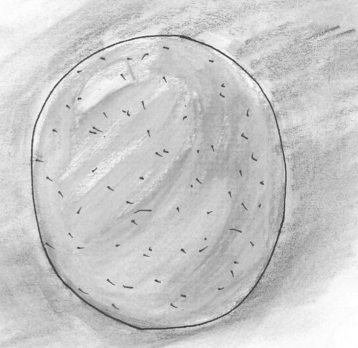

"Good idea, Jarrell," his mom said. "And maybe every now and then we can have cakes or candy, pie or ice cream, cookies or cupcakes."

"Okay, Mommy," said Jarrell with a smile, "but not too much. I need my fruits and vegetables so I can grow strong and healthy."

The End

"Hello, boys and girls. Jarrell and I have a great song about good foods to eat. Will you sing with us?"

Veggies and Fruits

Apples, bananas, oranges, and peaches.
Strawberries, grapes, all are delicious.
Carrots and peas, more salad please.
Veggies and fruits keep me strong and healthy.

For the Vitamin B's, eat carrots and peas.
Tomatoes and spinach and bananas are good for me.

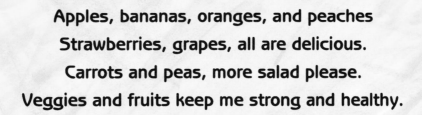

Apples, bananas, oranges, and peaches
Strawberries, grapes, all are delicious.
Carrots and peas, more salad please.
Veggies and fruits keep me strong and healthy.

Sweet potatoes and broccoli,
Oranges and peaches, have
Vitamins A and C.

Apples, bananas, oranges, and peaches.
Strawberries, grapes, all are delicious.
Carrots and peas, more salad please.
Veggies and fruits keep me strong and healthy.
Veggies and fruits keep me strong and healthy.
Veggies and fruits keep me strong and healthy.
Let's eat!

Download the Veggies and Fruits song at www.dijarodesigns.com

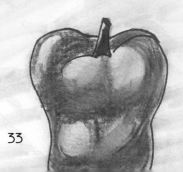

33

LaVergne, TN USA
11 March 2010
175622LV00002B